Granddad's Fish Tank.

Written and illustrated by

Adrienne Body

2014

My Granddad's fish are

the best fish to me.

Better than all

of the fish in the sea.

There's Danny MacDoogle

with googly eyes,

Freddy the fish is a
frisky wee fellow,
his fins flish and flash

in a fabulous yellow.
"Hello and good morning!"
he says to his friend,

then swims round in a circle

and says it again.

The sucker fish,

Mark,

has the ickiest task

of licking the

slimy bits

off of the glass.

He chomps

and he chews

a track through the grime.

It's a good thing he loves

the taste of the slime.

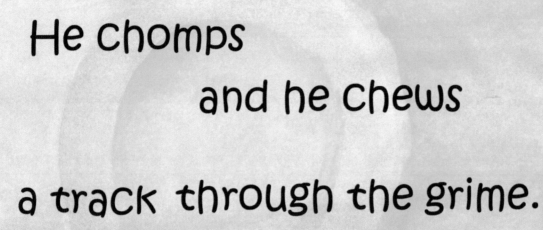

The squid that's named Kai
is all slippery and sly.

He spends most of his time
as a secretive spy.

 He hides
behind rocks

and among
all the weeds,

constantly watching

for dastardly deeds.

Sammy the snail
    is so sluggish and slow

he always forgets
        where he wanted to go.

So he goes up

and then down,

then left

and then right,

just to-ing and fro-ing
well into the night.

Gary the guppy
is grumpy and mean,

the angriest fish
that you ever have seen.

He spits in your eye
when you give him his food,

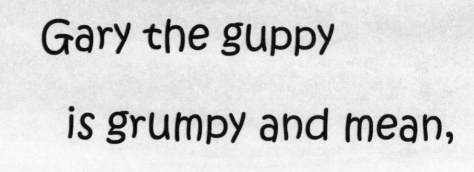

he's only content
being nasty and rude.

The fish that's named Ted
likes to mess with your head,

he floats on his back
and pretends to be dead;

and Seymour the seahorse
is a curious thing,

his unusual tail
is coiled like a spring.

But Barry the

blowfish is the

weirdest of all,

he puffs himself up

like a big spiky ball.

Chloe the clownfish
is always in trouble,

getting lost and confused

as she swims
through the bubbles.

The axolotl
named Greg
has four little legs,

and the crab
that's called Chuckles,
he skittles and scuttles.

The octopus Squiggles,
she gives me the giggles,

the way that her tentacles

wiggle and wriggle.

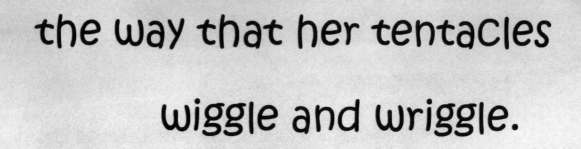

And perhaps,

if I'm good,

when it's time to go home...

... my Granddad will give me a fish of my own.

More books
by Adrienne Body

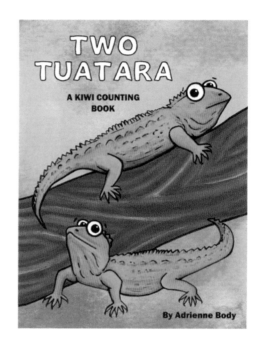

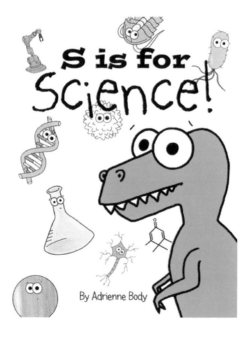

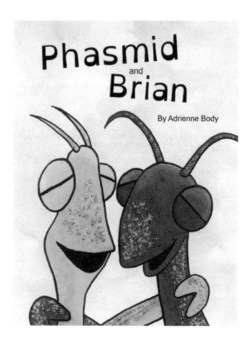

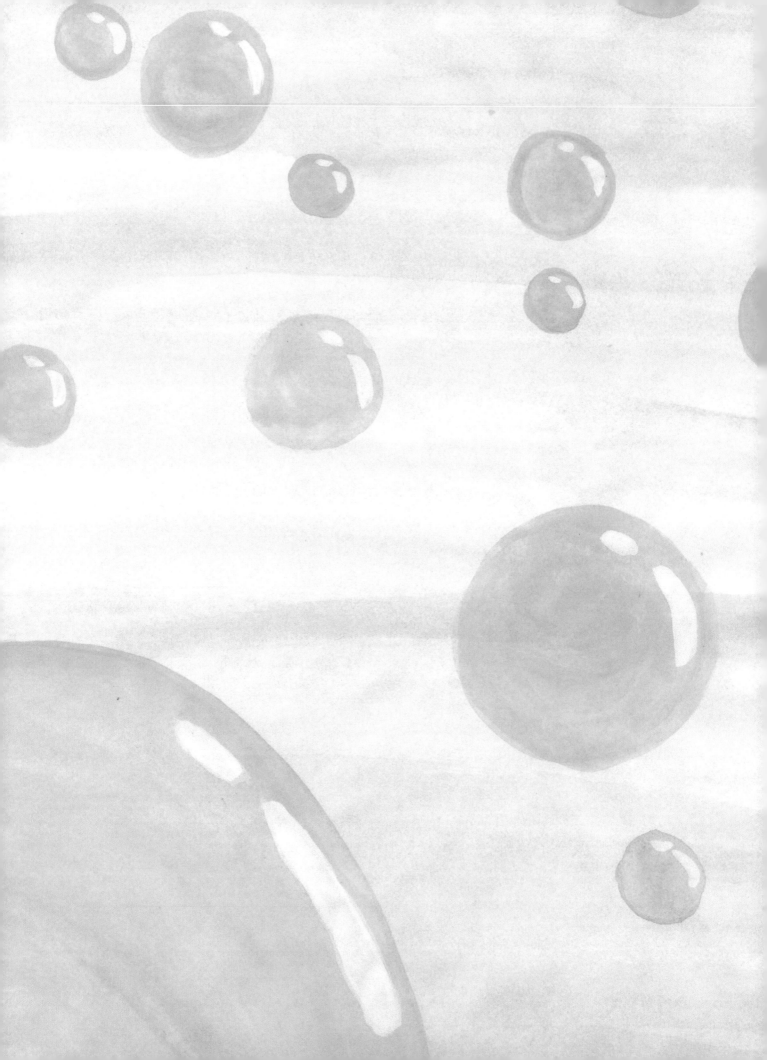

Made in the USA
Lexington, KY
16 June 2016